100% OFFICIAL

POPPY PLAYTIME ™

ORIENTATION NOTEBOOK

ORIENTATION NOTEBOOK

Scholastic Inc.

Playtime CO.

All rights reserved. Published by Scholastic Inc., *Publishers since 1920*. SCHOLASTIC
and associated logos are trademarks and/or registered trademarks of Scholastic Inc.

The publisher does not have any control over and does not assume any responsibility
for author or third-party websites or their content.

This book is a work of fiction. Names, characters, places, and incidents are either the product
of the author's imagination or are used fictitiously, and any resemblance to actual persons,
living or dead, business establishments, events, or locales is entirely coincidental.

ISBN 978-1-339-01495-1

10 9 8 7 6 5 4 3 2 1   24 25 26 27 28

Printed in China   38

First printing 2024

Book design by Dynamo

Special thanks to Seth Belanger, Zach Belanger, Isaac Christopherson,
Micah Preciado, Zachary Preciado, Brinna Ball, Anna Sorsby, and Eric True.

Orientation
Notebook

I RECEIVED THIS BOOK A FEW MONTHS AGO. I WAS CURIOUS WHAT THEY'D SAY, AND WHAT THEY WOULDN'T, SO I READ IT COVER TO COVER. THIS COMPANY IS FUNNY, IN THAT WAY, ONLY HANDING ME A BOOK LIKE THIS A FEW YEARS IN. I STILL DON'T UNDERSTAND WHY THEY HIRED ME, A BIOLOGIST, TO DO RESEARCH AND DEVELOPMENT AT A TOY FACTORY. THEY SAID I HAD EXACTLY THE SKILLS THEY WANTED, BUT THEY WERE VAGUE ABOUT WHAT EXACTLY THEY WANTED MY SKILLS FOR . . .

I'VE BEEN AT PLAYTIME A WHILE NOW, AND IT TURNS OUT THERE'S A LOT OF STUFF THEY DO HERE THAT ISN'T IN THE HANDBOOK. SO I'M ADDING A FEW NOTES OF MY OWN. THIS COMPANY IS NOT WHAT THEY MAKE IT OUT TO BE.

-P. W.

Playtime Co.

message from our founder

I am thrilled to extend a warm welcome to each and every one of you as you embark on an exciting journey with us at Playtime Co.! As the founder of this incredible company, it fills me with immense pride to see our family grow and flourish. Playtime Co. was established with one mission in mind: to bring joy and laughter into the lives of children around the world through the creation of high-quality, innovative toys.

Over the years, our humble factory has blossomed into a world-renowned institution, capturing the hearts of millions. Our dedicated team of designers, engineers, artists, and dreamers work tirelessly to craft toys that not only ignite imagination but also inspire innovation and exploration. From whimsical stuffed animals to mind-bending puzzles, every product that leaves our factory is a testament to our unwavering commitment to excellence.

At Playtime Co., we strongly believe that the true magic lies within our people. Each one of you brings a unique set of talents and perspectives, and it is through collaboration, creativity, and teamwork that we can continue to shape the future of play. As a member of our team, you are part of something extraordinary, and your contributions

will have a direct impact on the lives of children across the globe. We look forward to everything you'll do and accomplish here.

And remember, envision that future you desire, and never loosen your hold on it. Because even something so simple, so small as a toy, can change the future if it makes even one child feel less alone. Do this, and before you know it, you'll live that brighter future. All it takes is time. So, what's the time?

"PLAYTIME!"

Elliot Ludwig

Elliot Ludwig
Founder & CEO

A GREAT AMERICAN COMPANY

Playtime Co. was founded in 1930 and became the most renowned toy manufacturer in the world. Today, we're still known for our commitment to quality and our mission to bring joy to children everywhere.

Although we've created many widely beloved toys, such as Bron, Candy Cat, and Poppy, it was the release of Huggy Wuggy in the 1980s that took us to new heights.

How does a company that's more than six decades old stay ahead of the market? **Innovation is key.** We never fall back on past glories—we're always looking to the future!

But we also believe the history of this factory means something. While other companies move their factories overseas to reduce costs, Playtime Co. is a proud American company and will always manufacture its toys right here in the United States.

You may have heard rumors about problems at Playtime Co.—that our profits are declining and our new ideas aren't working, and even that dangerous incidents have occurred at the factory. This nonsense is put out by our rivals and disgruntled ex-employees. Don't believe it and please don't repeat it.

You're joining a company that's on the up. The future is bright, and we believe the 1990s will be our most successful decade yet!

YEAH, RIGHT. KEEP TELLING YOURSELF THAT.

EMPLOYEE GUIDELINES

Playtime Co. runs on a set of principles we like to call:

Fundamentally

Understanding the

Need

For

Awareness

Cleanliness

Timeliness

Obedience and

Regulating

Yourselves

See, even our rules are **FUN!** But not if you break them.

We expect **cleanliness** and we don't just mean keeping the factory clean. We want **you** to be clean. **Always** wash your hands before going onto the factory floor.

THEY CAN BE VERY WEIRD ABOUT THIS! RANDOM INSPECTIONS TO MAKE SURE EVERYONE'S FINGERNAILS ARE CLEAN, THAT KIND OF THING.

Stay at your station until the bell rings for the end of your shift, unless you have permission from a supervisor. Note that it is company policy **not** to allow overtime.

We take **safety** very seriously. If you suffer an accident at work, it cannot be our fault because we're so careful about safety—it must be that **you** are not being careful enough.

Our **surveillance system** is important to safety, and any attempt to interfere with it will result in termination of your employment. We watch everything you do because we **care**.

OF COURSE, THE DOWNSIDE TO SPYING ON EVERYONE ALL THE TIME IS THERE ARE **LOTS** OF VIDEOTAPES OF WHAT GOES ON AT THE FACTORY. OFFICIAL POLICY IS TO RECORD OVER THEM AFTER THEY'RE REVIEWED, BUT SOMETIMES A COPY OF SOMETHING THEY DON'T WANT ANYONE TO SEE SLIPS THROUGH THE NET. I'VE JOTTED DOWN SOME STUFF I'VE FOUND OUT FROM THESE TAPES.

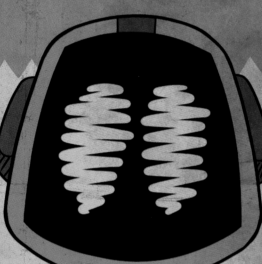

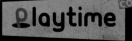

All our products and the processes used to make them are safe.
So if you experience:

- **Hallucinations**
- **Dizziness**
- **Disorientation**
- **Sudden vomiting**
- **Symptoms of schizophrenia**

Don't worry! The effects wear off and will not have long-term side effects.

However, you should report any such symptoms to your supervisor. Please make **very sure** you haven't reported it to a hallucination of your supervisor.

We are an **innovative** company, and that means you may see things while working here that seem strange, or impossible to understand. If this happens, **don't worry!** This is just how we try out new ideas, and it will all make sense eventually.

Like any company, information about what we do is valuable to our rivals, so we ask you **never to talk about what goes on in this factory to anyone**. They don't need to know, and it's better all around if they don't! Remember the non-disclosure agreement (NDA) you signed before starting work here.

And, in fact, **don't talk to one another unless strictly necessary**. Chatter and gossip on the factory floor is distracting and can result in harmful rumors being spread. We urge employees to be as silent as possible. If you like to whistle when you work, don't!

We expect **Loyalty** from our employees. If you're asked to do anything, don't ask why—just do it! If it wasn't necessary, we wouldn't be asking.

It's very important you **respect clearance levels**. We will decide what you do and don't need to know to do your job. There will be consequences for anyone snooping into areas they don't have clearance for—you may lose your job, or worse!

If you see anyone breaking company rules, or acting in a way that might work against the company's interests, **report it to a member of the security team at once**. A lot of our most valued employees got where they are today by reporting on their colleagues!

Don't forget, it's a rule that you must report any rule-breaking you see. **A failure to report rule-breaking** is against the rules, and you can be reported for it!

We have a lot of visitors coming through the factory, and when you see visitors, remember **you represent the company**. You represent **decades of tradition and excellence from one of the world's leading brands**. No pressure!

And above all, while you're working hard, safely, secretly, silently, and in complete obedience of these rules, don't forget to **have fun!** We like to think the spirit of fun inside our factory can be felt in every toy we make.

If you need a refresher on these rules, please refer to the **Employee Safety Rules** informational videotape.

MEET THE TEAM

ELLIOT LUDWIG

FOUNDER

The man who started it all. A good old-fashioned all-American, his brilliance and determination made this company what it is. Playtime Co. wouldn't be here without Elliot. His death saddened us all, but he remains an inspiration and the company continues in his memory.

LEITH PIERRE

HEAD OF INNOVATION

Innovation is key here at Playtime Co., and Leith understands that tradition better than anyone. What will toys look like in the twenty-first century? That's the question we're asking, and Leith is determined to answer it. He drives his team hard, but he gets results!

I ACTUALLY HAVEN'T MET MOST OF THEM. WE VERY RARELY SEE THE HIGHER-UPS. OCCASIONALLY WHEN THINGS GO WRONG, THEY PUT IN AN APPEARANCE.

LEITH HAS BEGUN TO TAKE OVER: THINKS HE'S CARRYING ON ELLIOT'S WORK, HIS TRADITIONS . . .

STELLA GREYBER

HEAD OF PLAYCARE

Stella is the real heart of this company—she might just have the greatest job in the world! Between her roles at Playcare and the Game Station, she's in charge of helping our orphans play games and have the time of their lives. It's like never having to grow up! (Please note that working in the Game Station requires you to be a responsible adult.)

TAKE EVERY STEP

PLAYCARE

LIKE IT'S YOUR LAST

WARNING: Serious injury or death may occur while standing near heated equipment. Please proceed through this area with extreme caution.

Playtime

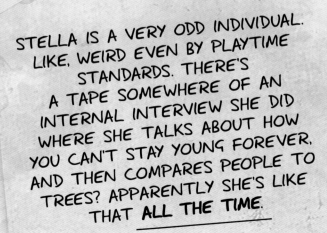

STELLA IS A VERY ODD INDIVIDUAL. LIKE, WEIRD EVEN BY PLAYTIME STANDARDS. THERE'S A TAPE SOMEWHERE OF AN INTERNAL INTERVIEW SHE DID WHERE SHE TALKS ABOUT HOW YOU CAN'T STAY YOUNG FOREVER, AND THEN COMPARES PEOPLE TO TREES? APPARENTLY SHE'S LIKE THAT **ALL THE TIME**.

EDDIE M.N. RITTERMAN

HEAD OF RESEARCH

Eddie has been working on new facilities here at the factory. We can't tell you much about what he's working on—he doesn't always tell **US** much about it!
But we're sure it will lead to great things!

NO ONE HAS MET EDDIE, AS FAR AS I CAN TELL. EVERYTHING I KNOW ABOUT HIM IS JUST RUMORS. HE DOES EXIST, THOUGH . . . I THINK.

Playtime Co. employees are not permitted to leave until they have completed their daily tasks.

Jimmy Roth

CHIEF MARKETING OFFICER

In today's crowded marketplace it's tough to make your product stand out. Jimmy's marketing techniques have helped take Playtime Co. to the next level. Is he a genius? Some might say so!

JIMMY IS A GENIUS AT CONVINCING PEOPLE HE IS A GENIUS. ALL THE EXECUTIVE STAFF SEEM IMPRESSED BY HIM, BUT HE TAKES CREDIT FOR EVERYTHING. HE IS OBSESSED WITH PUTTING AN "EE" SOUND ON THE END OF NAMES. I ONCE HEARD HIM CLAIM IT WAS HIS IDEA FOR HUGGY WUGGY TO BE BLUE.

WONDER IF JIMMY'S REPUTATION WILL SURVIVE THE SMILING CRITTERS FIASCO. I DON'T EVEN KNOW IF THE CARTOON WAS HIS IDEA, BUT IT SOUNDS LIKE PURE JIMMY TO ME. YOU CAN BE SURE THAT IF IT HAD BEEN A SUCCESS, HE'D HAVE TAKEN THE CREDIT, BUT AS IT WASN'T, I'M SURE HE'S TRIED TO BLAME SOMEONE ELSE.

THERE'S NO ENTRY FOR DR. HARLEY SAWYER, HEAD OF SPECIAL PROJECTS, KNOWN TO MOST AS JUST "THE DOCTOR." HE'S HEADING UP THE BIGGER BODIES INITIATIVE AND THINKS HE CAN SAVE THE COMPANY. HE WON'T LISTEN TO ANYONE . . .

HUGGY® SAYS

Remember to take BREAKS!

Breaks longer than 10 minutes are not permitted.

Playtime

OUR PRODUCTS

All employees should be familiar with all our products, so please read this section of the guide carefully. Our popular characters are the personalities of the company, so don't think of them as products—think of them as **colleagues**!

Larger-than-life models of our characters are famous features of the factory. In the past, our employees have been asked, "What's it like working with Huggy Wuggy?" If this happens to you, say something like, "He's a fun, friendly guy who's always got your back!"

Whatever you say, please make sure it fits with the established persona of Huggy Wuggy, or whichever character you're talking about. Deviating from this could be hugely damaging for our brand. You must know these characters like they're your friends. Come to one of our Wuggy Workshops if you feel you need help with this.

It's vital to our corporate identity that people believe the Playtime factory is a place where magic happens. If anyone asks you about working here, tell them about the amazing connection we all have with these beloved characters, rather than the truth.

THE WUGGY RANGE

You'll know them already—they're everywhere!

HUGGY WUGGY

Launched in 1984, Huggy Wuggy was a huge hit with kids and has become our best-known toy. He's the friendliest, furriest fellow you could hope to meet. He always has a smile for everyone, and he doesn't talk much—he just likes to hug.

Our market research showed anxious kids respond well to a toy they can attach to themselves, so we designed him with Velcro pads on his hands. Once he hugs onto you, you can't lose him! And he can't lose you.

A recent survey said 87% of people who were asked what product they associate most with Playtime Co. named Huggy Wuggy. We believe that in the 1990s Huggy Wuggy will only get bigger!

QUALITY TESTER CHECKLIST:

- Do the Velcro pads work?

- Are Huggy's eyes and mouth the correct distance apart?

- Are Huggy's arms and legs of equal length?

HUGGY WAS A BIG PART OF THE BIGGER BODIES INITIATIVE . . . LITERALLY. I MADE SOME NOTES ABOUT HIM THAT YOU CAN FIND LATER ON.

KISSY MISSY

Due to the huge success of Huggy Wuggy, in 1985 we launched Kissy Missy, a female version of Huggy. She is officially Huggy Wuggy's "better half," but be aware this is just a figure of speech. It should not be taken to mean Huggy Wuggy is in any way bad.

Kissy Missy has <u>exactly the same</u> product specifications as Huggy Wuggy but with pink fur and lashes on her eyes. Aside from these two things, all components of Huggy and Kissy are identical and interchangeable at the production stage.

NOBODY EVER WENT BROKE MAKING THE SAME TOY AGAIN BUT IN PINK, HUH?

MINI HUGGYS

These were introduced as a lower-priced version of Huggy aimed at children with less pocket money. However, with four different colors (yellow, red, green, and blue) they are also extremely collectible. Additionally, they can be linked together to form a chain of Mini Huggys. The best part of this is there is **no limit** to the number of Mini Huggys that can link, so any child can—and should—always be encouraged to buy more.

THE LONG LEGS FAMILY

You'll get a kick out of these lovable creatures!

MOMMY LONG LEGS

This is a perfect example of how a product that doesn't seem right at first can become a huge success. We wanted to follow the Wuggy line with a different take on long-limbed toys and came up with Mommy. At first we didn't think she was going to work out, but after we tested her on our Playcare orphans, she was a huge hit! All the kids loved her* and we felt the whole world deserved to be introduced to Mommy Long Legs.

YEAH, THAT'S NOT QUITE THE WHOLE STORY . . .

We launched the toy in 1991, with stretchy legs made from Playtime Co.'s patented elastic plastic. Please note that the original guarantee—if Mommy's legs snapped you could send your toy to us for a free replacement—is no longer valid.

*Except the kids with a fear of spiders or the color pink.

FUNTIME FACT

If you gathered every Mommy Long Legs toy sold since 1991 and tied their legs together, they would stretch all the way to the Moon! But part of the chain would burn up in Earth's atmosphere, so don't try it.

THE LONG LEGS FAMILY

Family is such an important part of what we do at Playtime Co. and it's at the heart of our products. That's why we created the Mommy Long Legs and Family set, which packages Mommy with Daddy Long Legs and Baby Long Legs.

Note that Daddy Long Legs is **not** just a reskinned version of Mommy with a hat instead of hair. His body sections and hands are a different shape than Mommy's. So if you're working on the Long Legs production line, ensure you have the correct mold installed. One time we ended up accidentally making a batch of blue Mommy Long Legs. We had to sell them to China under a different name ("Lady Ice-Spider"), and we don't want to have to do that again.

You may notice Baby Long Legs does not have long legs. An early concept, where their legs would grow as they were fed, was abandoned as unworkable, and also kind of disturbing.

Mommy is caring and sensitive, Daddy is good at barbecuing and has a mustache. The Long Legs Family represents traditional family values—human family values, that is, not spider family values. Some spiders eat their own mothers after hatching, and that's not what we're about as a company.

THE SWAP-IMALS

They're a bit of this and a bit of that!

CAT-BEE

Cat-Bee is one of our recent success stories. She's a fusion of a cat and a bee. We did test more imaginative names, but Jimmy Roth advised us to go with the more direct approach, and as usual, he was right. When people hear "Cat-Bee," they understand exactly what she is.

Cat-Bee is playful and loving—look at her heart-shaped paw pads! A lot of people ask if she stings. The answer is, honestly, we never thought about it in that much detail.

Cat-Bee is so popular with kids, we've made her the product they can manufacture for themselves in the Make-A-Friend room.

PJ Pugapillar

Following the same "pet and insect" formula as Cat-Bee, we created PJ Pugapillar. Whereas Cat-Bee is more cat than bee, PJ is more caterpillar than pug.

PJ loves games. He's like those dogs that follow you around hoping you'll play with them! We made him part of the Statues games in the Game Station for this reason.

Please note that PJ's body has **twenty-two** segments, which means **forty-four** legs. Quality control checkers on the PJ production line should count these segments and ensure no PJ is shipped with too many or too few. You might think kids don't notice this stuff, but trust us, they do, and they send us letters.

SMILING CRITTERS

Our most ambitious line yet!

Elliot Ludwig has never been a man to coast along on one success—he always wants the next thing to be bigger and better. So even as Huggy Wuggy became the nation's favorite toy, he was planning the next thing, and that was Smiling Critters.

The Critters are a group of animal friends, each with a distinctive color and a symbol they wear on a pendant. Each has a clearly defined personality, designed to express the values Elliot believed in. We're very proud of this line, and we feel it was creatively very successful.

AH, COMPANY SPIN AT ITS BEST. SMILING CRITTERS WAS A DISASTER. WE WERE DOING GREAT — THE HUGGY WUGGY MILLIONS WERE ROLLING IN — AND THE BOSS DECIDED TO PUT ALL THAT MONEY INTO LAUNCHING SMILING CRITTERS. EVERYONE WAS SURE THESE THINGS WOULD BE A HIT, AND WE HAD HUGE SALES TARGETS!

THE PROBLEMS STARTED WITH THE CATNAP CONTROVERSY, WHICH WAS ALL OVER THE NEWS THAT SUMMER. IT WAS MEANT TO BE OUR BIG TOY FOR CHRISTMAS, BUT WE HAD TO TAKE IT OFF THE MARKET. WE TRIED TO PUSH THE REST OF THE LINE, BUT IN TERMS OF THE COMPANY'S REPUTATION, THE DAMAGE WAS DONE.

THE CRITTERS CARTOON

Bringing our toys to life!

To make sure the Critters' personalities were known by the target market, Playtime Co. embarked on its most ambitious marketing campaign yet, funding the production of the *Smiling Critters* cartoon series, which aired on Saturday mornings during the summer of 1989.

The show combined wild and wacky adventures with a strong moral message for its young audience, and we were very satisfied with how it turned out. As it was principally designed to support the launch of the toy line, it was never intended to run for more than one season.

YEAH, RIGHT! IF THE SHOW HAD BEEN A HIT, YOU CAN BET IT WOULD STILL BE RUNNING TODAY AND THE MOST POPULAR CHARACTERS WOULD HAVE THEIR OWN SPIN-OFF SERIES AND THERE'D BE DIRECT-TO-VIDEO "MOVIES" THAT TURNED OUT TO BE ONLY FIFTY-EIGHT MINUTES LONG.

THE SHOW SUFFERED BECAUSE OF THE PROBLEMS WITH THE TOY LINE, BUT THE SHOW ITSELF WAS NOT LIKED, EITHER. CATNAP WAS MEANT TO BE THE CALM, REASSURING HEART OF THE GANG, BUT AUDIENCES DIDN'T LIKE HOW HE NEVER SPOKE, WAS DISTANT FROM THE OTHERS, AND HOW HE PUT THE REST OF THEM TO SLEEP AT NIGHT. PLAYTIME CO. RESPONDED BY POINTING OUT THE OTHERS WANTED HIM TO PUT THEM TO SLEEP. THAT SEEMED TO FREAK KIDS OUT EVEN MORE!

IT'LL NEVER BE REPEATED. PLAYTIME PUT IT IN THE VAULT. BUT THERE'S A THING CALLED AN "INTERNET BULLETIN BOARD" WHERE PEOPLE WHO RECORDED IT CAN GET IN TOUCH WITH ONE ANOTHER AND SWAP VHS COPIES. COLLEGE STUDENTS LOVE IT, APPARENTLY.

CAT NAP KILLER?

Parents report toy cat causes kids to have intense nightmares.

A series of incidents where children have suffered unusual sleeping patterns has been linked to a new toy made by Playtime Co., famous for its Huggy Wuggy character.

In recent weeks, doctors across the country have noted a rise in parents reporting their children are suffering from <u>intense nightmares</u>. There seemed to be no obvious cause for this, until one family reported the problems had completely stopped after their child lost her new favorite toy on a day trip to the woods.

The toy in question was CatNap, a central character in Playtime's heavily promoted Smiling Critters line. Further research quickly showed a strong link between these sleep disturbances and ownership of

CatNap toys, leading to speculation they are caused by the scent the toy emits.

As yet, the link is unproven. Many concerned parents aren't waiting for an explanation and are throwing their CatNap in the trash—and urging others not to buy the toy.

THIS IS THE KIND OF THING THAT LED CATNAP TO BE TAKEN OFF THE MARKET.

MEET THE GANG

They're charming and smell great, too!

Each character has a charm symbol and a scent, reflecting their personality. The idea behind the Smiling Critters was any child should be able to find at least one character they really relate to and could have a special bond with. But that shouldn't stop them from buying the others, too!

CATNAP

CHARM: Crescent Moon
SCENT: Lavender
CatNap never speaks but is a reassuring presence for the others and puts them to sleep at the end of the day.

DOGDAY

CHARM: Sunshine
SCENT: Vanilla
DogDay is very much the leader of the group, and where CatNap is silent and reserved, DogDay is energetic, upbeat, and welcoming. He represents values of friendship and support.

IS IT JUST ME OR IS THE LEADER ALWAYS THE MOST BORING ONE? HE DOESN'T GET TO HAVE A SPECIALTY. HE'S JUST THE MAIN GUY.

BUBBA BUBBAPHANT

CHARM: Light Bulb
SCENT: Lemongrass
Bubba Bubbaphant is smart and knowledgeable, and we wanted him to represent the value of studying and reading. He often makes interesting observations and loves to share his knowledge with his friends—whether they want to hear it or not!

HE KNOWS STUFF BUT PEOPLE DON'T WANT TO HEAR IT? YEAH, I CAN RELATE TO THAT.

BOBBY BEARHUG

CHARM: Heart

SCENT: Rose

Bobby BearHug is caring and loving, and whenever any conflict is brewing among the gang, she's the first one to remind them all what great friends they really are. She loves hugging and will always suggest activities that involve everyone and help build bonds among them.

HOPPY HOPSCOTCH

CHARM: Lightning Bolt

SCENT: Peppermint

A real tomboy, Hoppy Hopscotch can be a handful to deal with—she's impatient and can be loud. But she's also energetic and positive and is a big motivator behind the gang's activities. She's designed to show the value of getting out of your comfort zone and trying something new.

KICKINCHICKEN

CHARM: Star

SCENT: Ylang-ylang

KickinChicken is all about having fun and being active. He's a skilled skateboarder and a very cool customer, but underneath that hip exterior, he scares easily! He faces down his fears with the help of his friends.

WITH FRIENDS LIKE CATNAP, I'M SURPRISED HE FOUND ANYTHING ELSE TO BE AFRAID OF.

CRAFTYCORN

CHARM: Color Wheel

SCENT: Jasmine

The artist of the group, CraftyCorn can be a little shy and awkward when talking to others—it's in her art that she truly expresses herself! She's all about creativity and seeing the beauty in ordinary things.

PICKYPIGGY

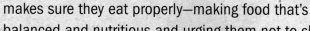

CHARM: Apple

SCENT: Citrus

PickyPiggy loves food—preparing it and eating it! While her friends go about their busy daily lives, Pig makes sure they eat properly—making food that's balanced and nutritious and urging them not to skip meals.

The Smiling Critters line is undergoing an overhaul at the moment. We think it's clear many of the characters could support their own product lines: PickyPiggy-branded snack foods, CraftyCorn-branded art supplies, Bobby BearHug–branded family therapy services, etc. We still have great plans for these guys!

THE COMPANY SANK SO MUCH MONEY INTO THIS THING, THEY COULDN'T ADMIT IT FAILED. BUT THERE WAS A LOT GOING ON WITH SMILING CRITTERS ON THE EXPERIMENTAL SIDE, TOO . . .

HERITAGE PRODUCTS

Meet the toys that made this company great!

POPPY PLAYTIME

Poppy was launched in 1950 and really put this company on the map. Talking dolls had been around for decades, but Poppy was different. She wasn't just a talking doll—she was also a **Listening** doll.

When Poppy was first launched, people couldn't believe that you could talk to her and she would talk back. But it was true. They all wanted to know how we did it, but the technology remains a closely guarded secret to this day!

IT SURE IS CLOSELY GUARDED. THEY MADE ME SIGN MULTIPLE NDAS SAYING I'D NEVER TALK ABOUT IT. I DON'T EVEN KNOW HOW IT WORKS. I ASKED SOMEONE ONCE AND SHE TOLD ME, "IT'S SIMPLER THAN YOU'D EXPECT," AND REFUSED TO SAY MORE.

We made clear in the instructions that if Poppy was dismantled by untrained personnel, she would break and no refund would be offered. That seemed to discourage people from poking around inside their Poppy doll.

Poppy was the perfect companion for lonely children—a sweet, perky little girl who could never be mean or spiteful and would always listen to your problems and offer a kind word in return. If you had Poppy, you didn't need anyone else, not ever!

Poppy was originally priced at $5.99—that's about $36.00 in today's money!—but being so cutting-edge, she was a premium product that people were willing to pay for. Especially for busy working parents who didn't have time to talk to their children. We sold **a Lot** of Poppy Playtimes to them.

BRON

Dinosaurs were big in the 1960s—well, they were always big, but you know what we mean—and Bron really took off when we launched him in 1961. Market research told us a brontosaurus would be a popular choice, and they're less difficult to make than those dinosaurs that have horns or plates on their back. He's a cuddly, lumbering sort of guy with a wry sense of humor.

BOXY BOO

Boxy Boo was a mischievous fellow we brought to the market in 1966. He's a jack-in-the-box with a difference: Not only did his head spring out of the top of the box, but his arms and legs also sprang out of the sides, offering more play possibilities. Boxy has since been discontinued, but we might rework him to bring him into the 1990s.

Progress Report.
EXPERIMENT 1199

Subject

Thomas Clarke, a fifty-nine-year-old employee of Playtime Co. since 1955, volunteered as an experimental subject following his unfortunate diagnosis of lung cancer. All paperwork has been logged, confirming he made this decision himself and was of sound mind.

Observations

The Bron model was thought to be an appropriate container, and the transfer seemed successful. However, Subject 1199 seemed more disorientated than expected, and his mental performance was disappointingly poor. He appeared not to understand what had happened to him.

More interestingly, but even more problematically, the other experiments were hostile to 1199. They knew he was different from them and attacked him. His thyroid and larynx were torn out, and he would have been killed had we not intervened and performed life-saving surgery.

Conclusion

Subject 1199 is now kept separate from the others. We await advice on what to do with him.

OTHER LINES

CANDY CAT

In the 1970s there was a danger of our products seeming old-fashioned, so in 1979 we launched Candy Cat as a more free-spirited character with a mischievous, even rebellious side. She just loves candy! What made this design really successful was Candy's lolling tongue, which kids could roll up and put back into her mouth. Meanwhile, the hatch on her back meant you could literally stuff her with candy—or whatever you liked! She's still available to purchase in the Gift Shop today.

BUNZO BUNNY

Bunzo is a cheerful yellow rabbit who loves to celebrate birthdays and clashes his cymbals together when he's excited. This toy is equipped with the ability to remember up to eight birthdays and deliver greetings on the day itself. Kids love to freak out their family and friends when Bunzo tells them when their birthday is!

laytime BOOGIE BOT

NEW FOR CHRISTMAS 1993! From the people who brought you Huggy Wuggy, here's Boogie Bot, the cutest little robot you'll ever see! He loves music and he loves to party! But he also knows when it's time to stop partying and help with the cleaning. Order now as we expect VERY high demand for Boogie Bot!

boogie bot™ 1993

REJECTED DESIGNS

We don't always get it right! Here are some of the products we've developed that didn't make it to market.

SIR POOPS-A-LOT

This classy, dignified fellow came with his own toilet, but he was rejected after focus groups had an overwhelmingly negative response.

FUNTIME FACT
The designer who came up with this was fired!

KICK-ME-PAUL

The concept behind this orange spherical toy was that kids could hit or kick him. We could say this was rejected for being contrary to Playtime Co.'s brand values, but the truth was no one liked him. He was resubmitted under the name Push-Me-Paul and rejected again, because the name was not the problem.

DAISY

Daisy was a marionette in the form of a flower. During testing she made children cry, so naturally she was rejected. The last thing we want at Playtime Co. is for kids to be scared—we would **never** knowingly design a toy to be frightening. By the time this was discovered, Daisy had already been added to some of our branding, and we may try to revive the character in a less creepy form some day.

ALWAYS STICK WITH A BUD!

Excessive employee fraternization is looked down upon, all workplace relationships should be disclosed to HR.

ℒlaytime

THINK GREEN ♻

REDUCE REUSE + RECYCLE

Employee recycling habits must not impede Playtime Co. work flow.

ℒlaytime

DEFECT

OWEN THE OVEN

A kitchen play toy with a difference! Well, two differences: First, he had a lovably grumpy expression, but second, and more important, he was a fully functioning oven with a top temperature of 400 degrees Fahrenheit. He could be used to bake small cakes, mini pizzas, cookies, etc. Sadly, during testing several children received third-degree burns.

SUNNI BUDDI

Another flower toy. The issue here was that we never worked out what he was meant to do. He's just a flower in a pot.

SURPRISE HARE

This was planned as a toy in the pocket-money range, maybe with different colors and shapes to encourage collectability. However, it fell out of favor when we pivoted to larger toys.

PET STONE

Our design team insisted this was a genius idea, but focus groups just thought it was some kind of joke.

BARREL O'HUGGYS

We loved this extension of the Huggy brand! These barrels of small elastic Huggys could connect to form chains. Unfortunately, in testing we found kids would mistake the Huggys for candy, creating a choking hazard. A shame, but the customer is always right!

DEFECT

INNOVATION

We do things a little differently around here!

Our reputation as an innovative company is important to us. After all, we're the people who made Poppy Playtime. We're always working on smarter products—toys that do things you've never seen a toy do before!

But no experiment ever comes without a little risk, because after all, if we knew what was going to happen, it wouldn't be an experiment! Please don't be alarmed. We know what we're doing, and we always have everything under control.

THIS HAS BECOME A RUNNING JOKE AMONG MY TEAM. AS SOON AS ANYTHING GOES WRONG, SOMEONE WILL SAY, "EVERYTHING'S UNDER CONTROL!" WE USUALLY GET A GOOD LAUGH OUT OF THAT.

The important thing is not to venture into areas where these experiments are taking place, and then you never have to worry about them. They always say, what you don't know can't hurt you, and it's true! However, from time to time you may be asked . . .

C_____ ____ ____ _____ ___ _____ ___ _____ _____ sinus
e _ _ _____ _____ ____ nn _ __ __ _ __ __ _ _ _
r_____ _____ ___ us

THERE ARE A LOT OF THINGS I WISH I DIDN'T KNOW. **EXPERIMENTAL** DOESN'T COVER WHAT GOES ON INSIDE THIS FACTORY . . .

SOME SAY THE COMPANY HAS BEEN DOING THE BIOLOGICAL EXPERIMENTS FOR A LONG TIME, AND THAT'S WHAT MAKES ITS PRODUCTS UNIQUE. I THINK THAT MIGHT BE TRUE. I FOUND AN OLD FILM CALLED POPPY PLAYTIME MAINTENANCE AND WATCHED IT . . . I KIND OF WISH I HADN'T.

For those employees involved in our experimental programs, a separate handbook is available.

I WISH I COULD FIND A COPY OF THAT. NOT THAT THEY EVER PUT ANYTHING INCRIMINATING IN PRINT.

SO THE COMPANY WAS STRUGGLING AFTER THE SMILING CRITTERS DISASTER. PROFITS WERE WAY DOWN AND THERE WAS TROUBLE AT THE FACTORY. EMPLOYEES SAW THINGS THEY SHOULDN'T HAVE, AND THERE WERE ACCIDENTS LEADING TO LAWSUITS.

DR. SAWYER FIGURED WE COULD SOLVE ALL THESE PROBLEMS WITH AN EXPERIMENTAL PROGRAM. GIANT TOYS WITH A LIVING CONSCIOUSNESS. HE SAID HE COULD CREATE THEM, AND THEY'D WORK AT THE FACTORY.

I FEEL LIKE CERTAIN SENIOR EMPLOYEES SHOULD HAVE ASKED MORE QUESTIONS AT THIS POINT. BUT THEY WERE DESPERATE TO TURN THE COMPANY AROUND, AND THE DOCTOR GOT TO DO WHATEVER HE WANTED. HE HAD A NURSERY FULL OF ORPHANS, AND NO ONE WOULD KNOW IF ANYTHING HAPPENED TO THEM.

A reminder that under the terms of your employment with Playtime Co., you are not to discuss anything that happens inside the factory with anyone. If you thought you saw something odd or disturbing, perhaps something that might be of interest to law enforcement, it's important to remember that **no, you didn't**.

THE GRABPACK

Another great Playtime Co. innovation!

The GrabPack is here to make your job easier. In return, you must **respect** the GrabPack. Look after it and don't use it for anything it's not designed for.

The GrabPack was invented by Elliot Ludwig to help him in the factory as he got a little older, but it was so "handy" we rolled it out to all employees. In basic terms, it's a backpack with two extendable hands, which have multiple functions. It can be used to operate controls, fetch objects, and even connect electrical circuits. It can also open color-coded doors.

The green hand can store an electrical charge temporarily, so power can be transferred between outlets. The yellow hand is more specialized and will only be issued to employees who apply for one and are judged to require it for their work (for instance, employees who often need to reach high places). It launches the user into the air, and due to the obvious risks of this, it can only be issued to select employees after completing a course.

THE GRABPACK REALLY DOES COME IN HANDY, AND NOT JUST WITH DAY-TO-DAY WORK. WHEN EXPERIMENTS GET LOOSE, THE GRABPACK HAS HELPED US DEAL WITH A LOT OF TRICKY SITUATIONS!

Once you start using it, you'll wonder why every workplace doesn't have these GrabPacks! Well, it's because we patented the technology and don't let anyone else use it.

Visitors to the factory also get to use a GrabPack, so they feel like they're really part of the team! But they're not. They should only use their GrabPack for the Make-A-Friend machine. Orphans can use it in the Game Station.

REMEMBER:

BE SAFE WHILE USING YOUR GRABPACK!

Playtime Co. is not liable for any danger or bodily harm that may occur while using the GrabPack™.

Playtime

Don't let visitors operate heavy machinery with it and certainly don't let them fire it at one another. But most importantly, make sure a responsible adult from each tour party signs the standard waiver, which states, "Playtime Co. is not responsible for any injuries caused by the GrabPack."

GUIDANCE FOR GUIDES

We're open to all, for just a small fee!

Our tours have been a hugely successful part of Playtime Co.'s operations for several decades now. Not only are they a great source of revenue, but they also help our customers feel closer to us as a company, while also making it clear we have absolutely nothing to hide!

Tours take place on Wednesdays, Thursdays, and Fridays, and **never** at any other times. Some tour days will be unavailable at Playtime Co.'s discretion.

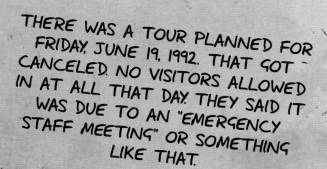

THERE WAS A TOUR PLANNED FOR FRIDAY, JUNE 19, 1992. THAT GOT CANCELED. NO VISITORS ALLOWED IN AT ALL THAT DAY. THEY SAID IT WAS DUE TO AN "EMERGENCY STAFF MEETING" OR SOMETHING LIKE THAT.

It's very important to keep tours strictly to the approved areas of the factory: the entrance, the main lobby, the Theater, the Make-A-Friend machine, and the Gift Shop. If a visitor sees something unauthorized, we have measures to deal with this situation, but it's much nicer not to have to use them!

If you're joining our tour-guiding team, you'll be getting specialized training in how to conduct yourself on tours, as well as the official history of the company.

WHICH ISN'T EXACTLY THE SAME THING AS THE ACTUAL HISTORY OF THE COMPANY.

Most of our employees will encounter tour parties at some point, and some of you will have tours coming through your part of the factory regularly. Do whatever it takes to make them happy! Except letting them use the factory equipment. Or playing on the conveyors. Or taking more toys than the ticket price entitles them to. Just use your common sense on this.

59

AROUND THE FACTORY

It's where the magic happens!

The Playtime factory can be a confusing place to navigate. It's pretty huge, and just when you think you've seen it all, you find another wing. But don't worry! We'll help you find your way around.

MAIN ENTRANCE

All visitors to the factory will enter this way. It's important they get a good first impression, so always put on a sunny smile in this area! Don't forget, you're on camera!

GIFT SHOP

This is located on the right-hand side of the entrance, so visitors can buy our products on their way out. Or their way in! There's never a bad time to buy Playtime Co. products! And remember, they don't have to be a gift—it's perfectly acceptable to buy things for yourself from the Gift Shop.

Note that the train that goes around the track suspended from the ceiling is just for display and not for sale. It's a very important part of the shop.

SECURITY OFFICE

This is located to the left of the entrance, and it is the base for our security operation. Suspicious visitors, or anyone suspected of stealing from the factory, will be escorted to this office. If you have anything to report, call the office and, if necessary, we'll bring you down here for an interview.

The door is protected with a color code. If you need this code, you'll be given it. Do not disclose the code to anyone, especially anyone who isn't a Playtime employee!

AUGUST 1995-SECURITY DOOR CODE:
GREEN
PINK
YELLOW
RED

GrabPacks are an important part of security because they are used to open and close a lot of the doors in the factory. So you may be brought to the Security Office to get training on how to use your GrabPack. Please pay attention to the informational tape! It costs money to make those things, you know.

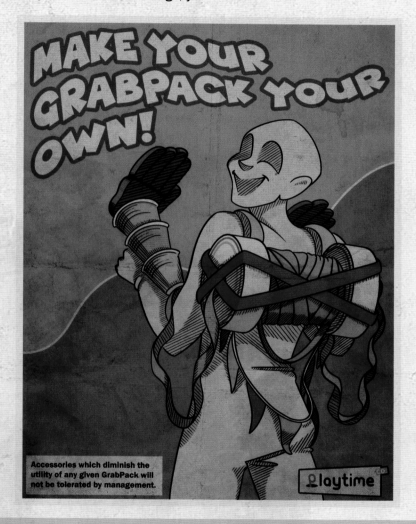

MAKE YOUR GRABPACK YOUR OWN!

Accessories which diminish the utility of any given GrabPack will not be tolerated by management.

Playtime CO.

Interested in a career in security?

We're always looking for more people. You'd be surprised how much security a toy factory needs! We can give you all the training you need to join our **retrieval team**. Drop by the office and ask for an application form.

LOBBY

The fun starts here! Visitors love seeing the giant Huggy Wuggy right when they enter Playtime Co. There are seven different doors leading off the room, and you'll walk through here every day as you move from one area of the factory to the next. Don't forget to say "Hi" to Huggy Wuggy as you pass!

Progress Report.
EXPERIMENT 1170

Observations

In appearances, everything seems to be working to schematic: Dense, stringy limbs that, when tested, even dented metal when swinging; teeth sharp enough to split bone, and a smile that says he's every bit the toy you believe you know.

Conclusion

We're very pleased with how this is proceeding. Undoubtedly this is the best product the Initiative has produced so far. He has good intelligence and does as he's told, so we have put him to work. He can hide right in plain sight. He can watch. Visitors would walk right by him, and they'd be none the wiser to his true nature.

This really bodes well for the success of the Initiative as a whole.

YEAH, SPOKE TOO SOON HERE. SEE THE REPORT ON THE NEXT PAGE.

Security Report.

Subject

In the evening of June 18, 1992, Subject 1170 escaped from the factory through a ventilation shaft. This was witnessed by two members of staff who raised the alarm at 10:27 p.m.

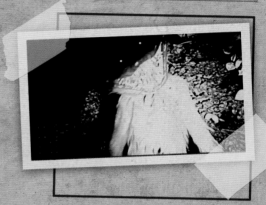

Event details

A retrieval team was mobilized at 10:30 p.m. Due to 1170's speed, he was almost a half-mile away by this time. However, we tracked him down in the forest. One member of the team attempted to subdue 1170 with tranquilizer darts after he rammed into his vehicle's windscreen.

At 10:38 p.m., 1170 was located at a railroad crossing. Again we fired tranquilizer darts at him, but he remained conscious. The effectiveness of our tranquilizers needs to be looked at. He escaped into the woods again, where he fed on deer. At 11:34 p.m., another member of the team located him.

2

Security Report.

The search radius was expanded to four square miles, including residential areas. At 3:38 a.m., cameras caught 1170 outside a house, where his intentions were unclear.

Aftermath

We finally caught 1170 and brought him back to the factory. Five members of the retrieval team were killed and another six have not yet been found.

THEY COVERED THIS INCIDENT UP AS MUCH AS THEY COULD. LEITH HIT THE ROOF. MY TAKE ON THIS IS SECURITY WAS LETTING HUGGY DO THEIR JOB AND GOT LAZY-AND FORGOT TO ACTUALLY WATCH HUGGY. WE HAD TO SHUT DOWN THE FACTORY TO THE PUBLIC ON SHORT NOTICE IN ORDER TO CLEAN UP.

POWER ROOM

Only maintenance employees should need to use this room. Your basic training should have covered what to do if you need to get the power back on in an emergency. **Do not** let visitors wander in here! Kids love to flick switches, push buttons, and stick their fingers in things.

ELECTRICAL INSTRUCTIONS

There are two sockets that can be connected by using your GrabPack. Just trail the cable around the two power poles to complete the circuit.

STORAGE AND SUPPLY

This area is mostly used for storing parts for the Make-A-Friend machine. Please try to keep the floor tidy! Tools and equipment can cause accidents if left lying around. Safety is so important to us here at Playtime Co.

The control panel on the walkway needs four fuses to operate. **Please** leave these fuses in the panel! If they're removed, they very easily get scattered across the floor and lost in corners. If you arrive in this room and find the fuses are **not** in the panel, please look for them and put them back where they belong!

CONVEYOR NETWORK

A lot of rooms in the factory are linked by conveyor networks.
These are designed for moving parts and products, not people!
Do not use them to get from one part of the factory to another,
and only enter them if you need to make repairs, move anything
that's gotten stuck in the system, or get the power back on.

Please do not let children get into the conveyor network during tours.
In the past, this has shut the factory down for hours while we track
down and retrieve young visitors from the system. Every tour should
include the words, "The conveyor network is not a ride!"

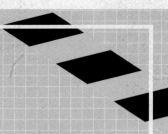

ELECTRICAL INSTRUCTIONS

1 If the hatch at the end of this conveyor is closed, the power will need to be restored, and it will be necessary to walk through the system.

2 Find an upward sloping belt you can climb. The slopes that are made up of rollers are impossible to climb, as you will just slide back down.

3 From the top of the slope, you will be able to see two sockets: the one next to the hatch and another one. Use your GrabPack to connect to the second of these sockets.

4 Slide down the left-hand side of the slope with the power post on it so your cable wraps around the post.

5 Return to the hatch and connect to the socket here.

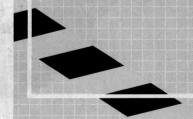

MAKE-A-FRIEND ROOM

This is the true heart of the factory. When it was built in 1960, this was the most advanced toy construction machinery in the world—a completely automated system—and it's still in use today. Invented by Elliot Ludwig, this machine is the pride of Playtime Co., and every visitor is brought here to experience the magic of pulling the three levers and watching their new best friend roll off the production line.

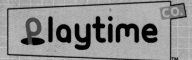

ELECTRICAL INSTRUCTIONS

1 The power system for the Make-A-Friend machine is located above it, in the walkways near the ceiling. Take care on these walkways, as there are sliding sections that should be moved into place before you walk across.

2 Connect to the first socket before you cross to the power poles; wrap your cable around the right-hand pole first and then the left-hand one.

3 Slide down the walkway so you can cross to the second socket. Be careful when crossing, as this will extend the GrabPack cable to its limit.

I DON'T KNOW HOW THOSE WALKWAYS PASSED A SAFETY INSPECTION.

Our motto for tours has always been "Nobody Leaves Without a Toy." You should make clear to any visitors that this only refers to leaving the Make-A-Friend machine room, not the factory. If they want to take the toy home, they will need to buy it at the Gift Shop.

However, to make sure no one forgets, we have installed a system on the exit that only opens the door when a toy is placed on the scanner.

Progress Report.

Subject

We've taken to calling this the Prototype. The team is amazed by how intelligent he is.

Observations

Problems have been encountered with the Prototype. Somehow, he managed to disassemble a digital alarm clock within his room and construct a laser pointer, which he then used to disable security cameras within his cell.

When the camera came back online, less than thirty seconds later, he seemed to have disappeared. He'd worked out where one of the camera's blind spots was and hid there. Our surveillance team worked this out and closed the door before he could escape.

IF YOU'VE EVER OWNED A DOG, YOU'LL KNOW IT'S EASIER TO MANAGE A DOG THAT ISN'T THAT SMART. IT'S THE CLEVER ONES THAT GIVE YOU TROUBLE!

2

Progress Report.

Conclusion

Unfortunately, one of the surveillance team was shut inside with the Prototype. We already knew the Prototype was violent, but what happened next proved it without a doubt. If you were to ask me why this happened, why he killed them, I'd say the Prototype simply did it because he wanted to, because he wanted blood, which for us is equal parts interesting, and terrifying.

WE SHOULD DESTROY HIM, BUT THE DOCTOR IS RELUCTANT! I THINK THE INTELLIGENCE OF THE PROTOTYPE MAKES HIM VALUABLE.

I DON'T KNOW WHAT THE PROTOTYPE WANTS.

STORAGE BAY

This area isn't used much. Don't take visitors here, even as a shortcut. It's a long way down from that walkway, and we don't want any more accidents. And be careful using your GrabPack in this area. There are always crates and stuff stacked around the place, and if you hit any of them with your GrabPack, it could easily bring them tumbling down on someone's head!

NOTHING IN THIS HANDBOOK IS ABOUT THE AREA BEHIND THE POPPY FLOWER THAT'S PAINTED ON THE WALL. NO ONE IS MEANT TO GO IN THERE. IT'S LIKE A HALLWAY IN AN ORDINARY FAMILY HOME, BUT IT JUST GOES ON AND ON. IT'S BASICALLY POPPY'S HOME. SHE'S IN THERE, INSIDE A GLASS CASE.

PEOPLE SOMETIMES TALK ABOUT POPPY IN THIS WEIRD SENTIMENTAL WAY, LIKE SHE'S THE COMPANY'S CHILD. BUT MOST OF THEM DON'T KNOW ABOUT THESE ROOMS . . . THAT SHE'S ACTUALLY HERE. I DON'T KNOW WHY SHE'S HERE.

THERE'S A PASSAGE THAT LEADS DIRECTLY FROM ELLIOT LUDWIG'S OFFICE TO THIS ROOM. I FEEL LIKE THAT MIGHT BE SIGNIFICANT? LIKE HE WANTED TO BE ABLE TO "VISIT" POPPY.

ELLIOT LUDWIG'S OFFICE

Our late founder's office is located in the center of a long hallway. You can't miss it; there's a plaque with his name over the door! Just think, this is the space where he generated the wonderful ideas that made this company great. But don't go in. Just think, and feel inspired.

This room is usually kept locked, but cleaning staff keep a key so they can get in to clean it. If you are cleaning staff, **DO NOT** move anything in this office. Just clean around it and keep the dust off. Everything is to be kept as Mr. Ludwig left it.

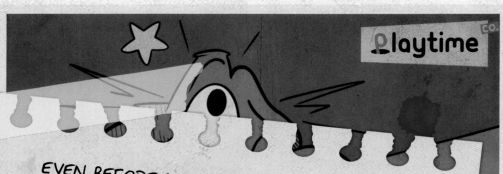

EVEN BEFORE LUDWIG DIED, I NEVER SAW HIM AROUND THE FACTORY. HIS OFFICE DOOR WAS ALWAYS CLOSED, BUT WAS HE IN THERE OR NOT? PEOPLE TALKED ABOUT HIM LIKE HE WAS STILL RUNNING THINGS, BUT IT FELT LIKE HE'D BECOME DETACHED FROM IT ALL.

Playtime Co encourag
to always exercise cau
moving throughout the

AFTER HE DIED, I WENT INTO HIS OFFICE, JUST ONCE, BECAUSE I WAS CURIOUS TO SEE IT FOR MYSELF. I WAS KIND OF SURPRISED HOW SMALL IT WAS, FOR THE OFFICE OF A CEO OF A BIG COMPANY. AND ISN'T IT WEIRD HE PICKED AN OFFICE RIGHT IN THE MIDDLE OF THE FACTORY, WHERE THERE ARE NO WINDOWS? JUST A VENTILATION SHAFT TO LET AIR IN.

MAINTENANCE CLOSET

This is just a space used by maintenance staff for storage. Check with them before you leave anything in here, otherwise it may be taken away and disposed of.

ELECTRICAL INSTRUCTIONS Playtime™

Making the connection between the power sockets in here is easier if you hit the higher one first, before wrapping the cable around the poles.

SENIOR STAFF ACCESS HALL

This room contains exclusive access routes for senior staff members. Use of these routes by unauthorized staff is a **disciplinary offense** and may result in termination of your employment. If you become aware of other staff members using these routes, report it to security immediately.

NAVIGATION ROOM

This leads to some of the factory's most exciting areas—Game Station, Innovation, Playplace, Research, and Production. It's a perfect place to go if you're lost and need to find your way back!

Th... ...ed mai ...and ...aff, ...ora... ...e ...th them b... ...av and ...os c...

IT WAS SOMEWHERE IN THIS AREA WE HAD ONE OF THOSE UNFORTUNATE INCIDENTS WHERE A STAFF MEMBER WITHOUT CLEARANCE SAW SOMETHING THEY SHOULDN'T. AN EMPLOYEE NAMED MARCAS BRICKLEY ENCOUNTERED A CREATURE HE DESCRIBED AS "FIFTY FEET LONG WITH A THOUSAND LEGS."

THIS ISN'T A TOTALLY ACCURATE DESCRIPTION OF PJ PUGAPILLAR, BUT WE THINK THAT'S PROBABLY WHAT HE SAW. LEITH ORDERED HIM TO FORGET ABOUT IT. IF HE TOLD ANYONE ABOUT IT, IT DIDN'T SEEM TO HAVE ANY CONSEQUENCES. I MEAN, WHO'D BELIEVE THAT?

SECONDARY POWER ROOM

The factory is a big place and uses a lot of energy, so another power room is needed. Some staff members have complained that connecting the sockets in this room is a little complicated, but it really isn't! You just have to remember that every time your GrabPack connects a socket to a power post, this will trigger a part of the walkway to shoot upward, and if the cable is in the way, then it will sever the connection.

ELECTRICAL INSTRUCTIONS

1 Stand on the left walkway, near the socket, and shoot your hand at the socket on the right, so your cable lies behind the blue pipe. This will keep it clear of the moving part of the walkway on your right.

2 Then go back up the walkway, keeping close to the barrier that's next to the blue pole, so you keep the cable clear of the moving part of this walkway.

3 Now go back to the walkway on your right and wrap your cable around the power pole here. Then you can cross over to the left and wrap it around the other pole. Go back to the platform on the right and make the final connection to the socket on the left with your other hand. See? Simple!

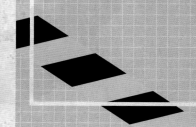

GAME STATION

This is a very special part of the Playtime factory, built specially for the orphans adopted by the company as part of our commitment to poor, unfortunate children. It contains several attractions and offers enough fun to forget the outside world. Mommy Long Legs is their guide here, making sure everyone is safe and having a great time!

Please note: Employees are **not** permitted to spend their breaks here, whether it is in use by orphans or not. If you see anyone using the Game Station without authorization, or holding parties here after hours, please report them to management.

Employees playing games that are meant for orphans to use makes Mommy Long Legs very sad!

The three levers on the train platform's control panel open up the Game Station areas.

REALLY CREEPY THAT ALL OF THESE PHOTOS WERE TAKEN AT NIGHT . . .

MEMBERS OF THE TOURS DEPARTMENT HAVE ASKED SEVERAL TIMES IF THEY CAN INCLUDE THE GAME STATION ON THE FACTORY TOUR, FIGURING IT'D BE A FUN WAY TO END THE DAY. THEY WOULDN'T ASK FOR THIS IF THEY KNEW WHAT IT'S REALLY ABOUT, OR WHO RUNS THE GAMES.

Progress Report.
Experiment 1222

Subject

Initially we believed Experiment 1222 was a failure, being too hostile to work with. But we have made careful observation of her manner and noticed how protective she is of the other experiments. She has a motherly nature we hadn't anticipated.

Observations

We have put her to work in the Game Station, looking after the orphans. This seems to be going well. She is kind to the kids and doesn't act out in front of them. She seems to enjoy the games, and her elastic limbs can stretch hundreds of feet, which is helpful in keeping a big crowd of kids under control.

Conclusion

The orphans have questions about what she is. They figured she isn't a puppet or a person in a suit. But we made a joke out of it, and we seem to have convinced them to accept her. The Doctor thinks it will be good preparation for what comes later.

Progress Report.
Experiment 1222

Update

Launching the Mommy Long Legs toy has helped the orphans warm to 1222. She's now more familiar to them. However, some employees in the Game Station have concerns over 1222's stability. She reacts badly if anyone cheats on the games, and she can get difficult when the orphans leave and don't come back. She has also been seen wandering around outside the Game Station, in areas where workers without clearance can see her. We had to put out an announcement about it.

THE OFFICIAL LINE WAS THAT IF SPIDERS LIKE THAT EXISTED, EVERYONE WOULD ALREADY BE DEAD. NOT SURE SOME EMPLOYEES FOUND IT AS REASSURING AS THEY'D HOPED.

MUSICAL MEMORY

This is the first game we provide for our orphans to play. It's a test of brain power, and it's also great fun! Kids must remember sequences of colors, shapes, symbols, and letters and push the right buttons in the right order. If they get it wrong, Bunzo Bunny will lower from the ceiling—oh no! If Bunzo reaches them, it's game over.

IF YOU'RE HELPING TO RUN THIS GAME, IT MAY BE USEFUL FOR YOU TO KNOW HOW THE ROUNDS WORK:

- The first round uses four colors: red, yellow, green, and blue.

- The second round adds violet.

- The third adds white and orange.

- The fourth round adds J, ♡, ?, π, and :).

- The fifth round is an extra-special challenge! It adds turquoise, G, ⚠, burgundy, Ω, θ, tangerine, λ, *, E, and more. It goes pretty fast, too! An emergency cancel button pops up so if the player is overwhelmed by this, all they have to do is hit the button.

I'M NOT SURE THE ORPHANS ACTUALLY FIND THIS FUN. I HEARD SOME OF THEM HAVE NIGHTMARES ABOUT IT, AND ONE SCREAMS IF YOU SAY A LIST OF COLORS TO HIM.

Note that the puzzle uses different sequences each time, so players can't solve it by watching someone else and remembering what they did. Don't let them help one another. We want to know how well they can do it! It's important.

STATUES

This game is an obstacle course with a twist: You're only allowed to step through it when it's dark! If the light comes on, you have to stop, or PJ Pugapillar will munch you down! (We advise Game Station employees to carry a flashlight at all times in case of accidents.)

Note that players don't have to stop moving completely and are allowed to look around. They're just not allowed to move their feet. When the lights come on, they should take the time to get their bearings and consider their next move!

THERE ARE FOUR SECTIONS TO THE STATUES COURSE:

- The first is a castle-style maze.

- The second is a series of rings with a pit filled with foam chunks underneath. Players can try to swing from the rings, which light up in the darkness. If they fall, the foam chunks will slow them down, and they may think they will be caught by PJ—however, PJ **only** catches the player if they move in the light.

- The third is a tunnel maze with three different openings: easy, medium, and hard. There's a special prize of a PJ Pugapillar statue for anyone who completes the hard route! (Don't tell the orphans, but the medium route is entirely pointless. We're just interested to see who picks it.)

- The fourth is another foam pit, this time with larger blocks for the player to jump between.

OBSERVERS OF THE GAMES CAN WATCH FROM THE VIEWING ROOM AT THE SIDE, WHICH HAS LARGE WINDOWS LOOKING OUT ACROSS THE PLAY AREA.

WACK-A-WUGGY

One of our most popular games, Wack-A-Wuggy is where you have to watch out for the Wuggys emerging from the pipes and whack them with one of your GrabPack hands. (The GrabPack storage room is conveniently located to the right of the Game Station.) Make sure the room is well-lit, as the game is very difficult in the dark!

Wack-A-Wuggy lets children take out their excess energy in a harmless way, helping to make the world a calmer place. Our scientists have studied this and confirm it to be the case. It helps our Playtime orphans grow into well-adjusted people.

ELECTRICAL INSTRUCTIONS

1 If you need to restore power to the Statues game, take the charge out of one socket and put it in the other to activate the grapple bar above you.

2 Use this grapple bar to get up and connect to the left-hand socket up here. Don't use your green hand as you'll need it for the next step.

3 Drop down to the floor, wrap around the power posts, and then activate the grapple bar again so you can get up and make the connection.

THESE ELECTRICAL INSTRUCTIONS MUST HAVE BEEN ADDED BY PEOPLE IN THE KNOW.

MOLDING ROOM

This is where we manufacture parts for the GrabPacks. Our orphans will need to use GrabPacks to play the games, but if their GrabPack is faulty, they may be upset or frustrated. So you can make it into an extra treat for them by bringing them down here to make a replacement hand themselves! At Playtime Co., we can always turn a disaster into a good time.

As well as manufacturing the green GrabPack hand in this room, we keep an informational VHS tape that explains what the hand does. Please watch this tape if you've never used the green hand before—it's a little different!

You can activate the equipment in here by pulling the lever on the wall, then use the control panel, hitting the buttons from right to left. Make sure the pipework is all operational as you go through the process.

If the machine runs out of paint, a light on the panel will flash and a sign on one of the machines will indicate NO PAINT. To refill the machine, climb the walkway that will take you up to the machine. You should find more paint on the conveyor belt, which you can put in the machine.

If you need to test the new hand, there's a green socket you can take the charge from and transfer it to the red socket.

REJECTED ROOM

This is where we keep products that were designed and developed but didn't meet Playtime Co.'s high standards. Don't include this room on tours—people don't want to see our failed ideas! But it's important we keep a record of these things so we don't repeat our mistakes. And who knows, sometimes yesterday's failed idea can inspire tomorrow's stroke of genius.

There's an elevator platform at the end of this room. Don't overload this platform! If anything too heavy is placed on it, the platform will not rise until the excess weight is removed.

If you do need to move anything heavy, this room is equipped with a crane that runs along a track on the ceiling. You can use your GrabPack to move this crane into position, and use the GrabPack's green hand to get power and transfer it to the crane.

Memo

From: Security
To: Human Resources
Re: Richard Lovitz

As you may know, Rich works in distribution and operates mainly around the storeroom. He has recently been overheard having conversations with fellow workers, which isn't an issue in itself, but we are unhappy with the content of some of these conversations.

While complaining of being unable to locate boxes of Huggy Wuggy toys, Rich allegedly said, "Nobody in this stupid company knows what they're doing." He went on to remark that the storeroom had been "flooded" with "orphanage junk."

We recommend that Rich be reassigned to the Rejected Room.

No punishment is necessary for <u>Avery,</u> who Rich was speaking to at the time.

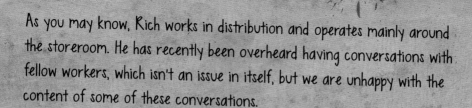

MAYBE HE WAS THE ONE
WHO REPORTED RICH.

ACCESS PASSAGES

These corridors are used for moving things around the factory. They can also be used to exit in an emergency, so please ensure nothing is left blocking them. Also, the power lift needs to be in good working order—we don't want people to get stuck here!

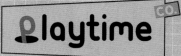

ELECTRICAL INSTRUCTIONS

1 If the power is off, you'll need to follow a particular sequence of steps to turn it on. This connection is awkward due to the particular architecture of this passage, so please avoid turning the power off if at all possible.

2 Connect to the socket in the corridor. When your cable makes contact with the power pole, the platform will start moving up, so hop on it before it goes too high.

3 The second power pole is up here, but you will not be able to get down or reach the other socket. So detach from the first socket and let the platform descend without you on it.

4 Crouch down, shoot your hand to the first socket again, and wrap around the higher power pole.

5 Jump back down, wrap around the lower pole, and connect to the other socket. The platform and door should now be operational.

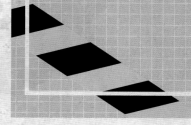

CART TRACKS

For faster transportation of items around the factory, we have a cart system. Again, visitors are to be reminded these carts are not for riding in. You can easily move carts around by using your GrabPack. Some of our employees have given names to the carts—they're such a quirky and creative bunch!

YEAH, IT COULDN'T BE BECAUSE THEY'RE BORED OUT OF THEIR MINDS, OR BECAUSE THE WEIRD ATMOSPHERE OF THIS PLACE IS DRIVING THEM SLOWLY INSANE.

Employees suffering from any sort of cardiac issues must ensure that management is fully informed.

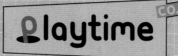

ELECTRICAL INSTRUCTIONS

1 A series of grills are installed on the tracks and in the corridors here for safety and security reasons. Some of these grills can be opened by using the green GrabPack hand to take and apply electrical charge.

2 By walking around the corridors, you can get onto the other side of the first two grills and open them up by operating the levers.

3 The third grill can be opened by powering up the sockets on either side of it. Get a charge from the first socket and bring it back to the final grill, but don't put it in either of the sockets by this grill.

4 Instead, power up the socket in the corridor to your right to open another grill, which has a powered socket behind it. Take the charge from this socket and put it in one of the sockets by the final grill. Then take the charge back out of the socket in the corridor and put that in the other one.

5 Remember, the charge doesn't last long, so you need to complete this task quickly or you'll have to start again.

WATER TREATMENT ROOM

The factory has its own water treatment facilities. **Do not** drink the water here or allow visitors to drink the water. Above all, **no swimming** is permitted in the Water Treatment Room. This is for your own good, as well as everyone else's.

Using the controls, you can rotate the two sections of walkway to make a bridge over the water tank to get where you need to go. It's very simple! Please do not hit the buttons repeatedly as the mechanism may be damaged.

The fa...
visitor
Room

Cont
tank
repe

The
vis
Rc

-U
tl

visito
Roor

Using
the wa
button

Has its
drink th
is for yo

YEAH, THIS HAPPENED. NOW THE BUTTON THAT ROTATES THE BOTTOM SECTION 90 DEGREES ALSO MAKES THE TOP SECTION ROTATE 45 DEGREES. SO IT'S IMPOSSIBLE TO MAKE A BRIDGE TO THE GAME STATION DOOR. NO MATTER HOW MANY TIMES YOU HIT THE BUTTONS, OR IN WHAT COMBINATION, THE TOP PIECE WILL ALWAYS BE IN THE WRONG PLACE.

I'M NOTING THIS SO I DON'T FORGET:

HITTING THE BUTTON FOR THE BOTTOM SECTION THREE TIMES WILL POSITION THE BRIDGE TO CROSS TO C2.

AFTER THIS, PUSHING THE TOP SECTION BUTTON ONCE, THE BOTTOM SECTION BUTTON TWICE, AND THEN THE TOP SECTION TWO MORE TIMES MAKES A PATH TO THE C4 DOOR.

Room C2

The production line for Bunzo Bunny runs through here, and Bunzo toys are carried along conveyors from one part of the factory to another. The buttons on the walls change the direction of the conveyors, but **only authorized personnel** should make adjustments to these conveyors. Otherwise, all our Bunzos could end up in the wrong places and **no one wants that**.

If you **do** need to send the Bunzos higher into the conveyor system, you can use the elevator to move up and down. The buttons will make the Bunzos go left instead of right, which will keep them in the system. The arrows clearly indicate which way the conveyors are running. Follow these instructions carefully:

- Stand on the elevator and push the first red button.

- Turn, reach up, and push the blue button with your GrabPack.

- Pull the lever and ride the platform up.

- Push the yellow button.

The red button at the top, to the left of the yellow pipes, will send the Bunzos into a part of the system where the conveyors don't connect up. If you send them here, they will fall off and become lodged in the pipes. If this happens, please take the elevator down and remove them. If you press the button above the gap in the conveyors, any Bunzo on that last conveyor will come back toward you.

The maintenance department has been informed about the gap in the conveyors. Many times.

SUBSIDIARY POWER ROOM

This can be found in the depths of the building. The factory certainly does use a **Lot** of power!

ELECTRICAL INSTRUCTIONS

1 Connect to the socket in this room with the blue hand of your GrabPack and wrap the cable around the left-hand pole.

2 This will bring down the cover over the powered-up socket, so you can charge the green hand of your GrabPack.

3 You can use this charge to get the power on in the next room, which will open the gate.

4 Now that the gate is open, reconnect to the first socket, wrap the cable around the two power poles, and connect to the socket behind the gate.

CONVEYOR OUTLET

This is just an access point for the conveyor system, but we tried to brighten it up a little by painting a nice picture of Candy Cat on the wall. The lever here activates the conveyor belt.

POWER ROUTING ROOM

This room is easy to identify by the four colored levers on the walls. You must operate these levers in the correct sequence. If you forget the sequence, use your GrabPack to grapple up into the ceiling and check the numbers on the battery packs:

1 = Red
2 = Blue
3 = Green
4 = Yellow

The door to this room will only open when the power is on.

INCINERATING ROOM

The furnace here has lots of uses! It's mainly for heating and shaping metal components, but it also helps heat the factory. And like any normal company, from time to time we need to burn stuff and ensure it's never seen again. If your supervisor or any senior member of staff asks you to burn something for them, don't ask questions! Just head down to the furnace and get burning.

And don't bring visitors down here, unless they're giving you a lot of trouble! Just kidding. But seriously, don't bring them down here.

Obviously don't walk into the furnace! But if you do somehow find yourself in there, stay at the far end of it until the flames die down, and you should be safe. Please note that Playtime Co. accepts no responsibility for injury sustained by employees who walk into the furnace.

MAINTENANCE NOTE

The main gear in the machinery here wears out easily. If you need to make a new one, the gear mold should be stored on a shelf. You can climb the steps to the mold slot on the molding machine and insert the gear mold into it. Use your green GrabPack hand to take a charge to the socket by the furnace, which will light it. Wait for the flame to die down, then take the new gear and insert it into the mechanism on the opposite wall.

Keep all parts of yourself and your GrabPack away from any heavy machinery. Dismemberment may otherwise occur.

Playtime co.

GRINDER ROOM

The grinder is used to break up large pieces of waste before they're disposed of, and whoa, it is **super** dangerous! When it's not in use, the power should be disconnected, because otherwise this is just a lawsuit waiting to happen. Anyone going near it risks getting their limbs caught in the grinder, which will draw them into it—a great way to get rid of anyone you don't want around! We're joking, of course. It would be a terrible tragedy if anyone got caught in the grinder.

SEWER SYSTEM

This is obviously a necessary part of the factory, but please **do not** use it as a way of getting from one part of the factory to another, **even if you are in a hurry**. There are grapple bars in this area, but they are only to be used in an emergency. Only use them if you have become stuck in the sewers by circumstances beyond your control.

BAY 09

This is located behind and under the Game Station and contains many essential pipes and wires. We are currently compiling a guide to what all these do and where they go, because we're not actually sure. Contact the maintenance team if you'd like to volunteer to help.

TRAIN STATION

The train is a joyous way to end any trip to the Game Station! Once the day's fun is done, orphans can be escorted onto the train and sent back to Playcare. As a security feature, the train can only be operated with the use of a unique code.

PLAYCARE

It's not enough to say you care, you have to show it!

Becoming one of the world's leading toy brands is all very well, but the achievement that makes us most proud is our Playcare program. The work we do here really makes a difference to the lives of children who otherwise wouldn't have had much of a chance in life.

Elliot Ludwig founded Playcare in 1976 with the aim of creating a state-of-the-art childcare system for orphans. It's a home that takes care of all their needs: play, education, and, if necessary, treatment for trauma. There's no need for them to leave—ever!

We hope to provide opportunities for our orphans to remain in the Playtime family and work at the factory. We strive to identify their potential and do what we can to help them achieve it.

Under the leadership of Stella Greyber, Playcare has shown continued success and is even more important to what we do at Playtime Co. Our Playcare orphans learn from us, and we learn a lot from them, too!

We're sure you'll understand the orphans' welfare must be our top priority, and so access to Playcare will only be given to employees who have passed our strict background checks.

THEY ARE VERY CAREFUL ABOUT NOT LETTING EMPLOYEES OUTSIDE PLAYCARE AND THE GAME STATION TALK TO THE ORPHANS. I GUESS IF EMPLOYEES GET TO KNOW THE ORPHANS, THEY MIGHT NOTICE WHEN ONE OF THEM SUDDENLY ISN'T AROUND ANYMORE.

Progress Report
EXPERIMENT 1186

Subject

Bobby BearHug: Smiling Critters Bigger Bodies Initiative

Observations

Three hours following awakening-observations:
Her body continues to spasm. Eyelids flutter. Paws twitch.

Subject doesn't seem to show any awareness of where she is. Could sensory functions be distorted, or altogether absent? We speak to her, try to get her attention by making sounds, but she does not register our attempts.

The auditory nerve in the ears directly communicates sound to the auditory cortex in the brain. It appears we may have failed at wiring the connective cords and might be forced to go back under the knife to fix this. A lack of response seems to indicate the necessity of this task.

It's clear that our procedures still haven't corrected issues with vocals, either. Her mouth moves, as if to speak, but nothing is said. We'll need to correct these processes with subsequent subjects if we're to potentially have these toys interact with our children.

Several hours after awakening, she tried to stand and walk to the other side of the cell but couldn't keep her balance. She looks to be searching for help, continuing to spasm.

She's trying to scream, but she has no voice. She's silent. I'm not sure if she knows she's not making any sound.

Conclusions:

Work will need to be done to perfect the Bigger Body formula we began with Boxy. Each iteration improves on the former. However, if we're to meet the goals of Dr. Sawyer, and produce Bigger Bodies subjects that we can integrate into a factory setting, then more work will need to be done.

As it stands, Bobby will require further experimentation. If we're to create Subject 1188 according to schematics, then each of these "Smiling Critters" will prove a good testing ground for ironing out these issues.

THE DOME

Growing up in a toy factory means you don't have a lot of outside space, so we made the Dome to compensate for that. The Dome's ceiling shows a bright blue sky in the daytime and changes to a moon and stars at night.

A generator, which powers the whole Playcare department, is housed in the ceiling. The control panel for this is concealed near the entrance of Home Sweet Home. (It's hidden so the orphans don't interfere with it!) Employees need the correct key access in order to use the elevator that takes them up to the Generator Room.

SMILING CRITTERS WAS ALL BOUND UP WITH THE BIGGER BODIES INITIATIVE AND ITS LINKS TO PLAYCARE. I WONDER IF THERE'S A LINK BETWEEN THE EDUCATION THE ORPHANS GOT IN PLAYCARE AND THE MESSAGES AND MORALS FROM THE CARTOON SHOW.

WE CREATED BIGGER BODIES VERSIONS OF EACH TOY IN THE SMILING CRITTERS LINE AND ASSIGNED THEM TO DIFFERENT PARTS OF PLAYCARE, AND THE FACTORY AS A WHOLE.

HOME SWEET HOME

Whenever the orphans are not engaged in organized activities like schooling or the Game Station, this is where they go to play, read, or sleep. There are separate boys' and girls' dormitories decorated in a Victorian style. The modern world is a hectic and dangerous place, so why not let our orphans grow up in a better, more simple time?

IT MAY BE RELEVANT HERE THAT ELLIOT'S WIFE DIVORCED HIM BECAUSE HE DEVOTED ALL HIS TIME TO THE BUSINESS. THERE'S ALSO SOMETHING ABOUT A TRAGIC DEATH IN HIS FAMILY . . . IT ALWAYS FELT LIKE HE WANTED TO HAVE A FAMILY WITHIN THE FACTORY, SO HIS WHOLE LIFE COULD BE HERE. I BELIEVE THE OPENING OF PLAYCARE WAS PART OF THAT, IN MANY WAYS.

Some of the children who live here have come from difficult backgrounds and have trouble getting to sleep at night, which can keep the other children awake. We create an environment where they are **guaranteed** a good night's sleep, leaving them fresh for the next day's activities.

"RED SMOKE"

Observations

The gas dubbed "Red Smoke" has been applied to the Playcare residents each night. The aim is greater than merely easing our counselors' workload by ensuring children sleep through every night. We also want to give them better quality sleep.

Our observations are very positive, suggesting sleep under Red Smoke not only gives more energy, but it also improves brain functions during sleep. Children show increased memory retention and better emotional processing of the day's events. This can help them achieve their potential.

Problems have been observed in a select few individuals, such as intense nightmares and sleepwalking accompanied by unusual heart activity, dilated pupils, severe hallucinations, chills, and nausea.

Conclusion

In light of these side effects, we have discussed whether or not to go on using Red Smoke. Opinions are divided, but the general feeling is the pros outweigh the cons.

TOY STORE

The orphans are permitted access to the Toy Store to select toys of their own, choosing from the full Playtime Co. range. Free choice and identification with particular characters is important.

Our older orphans may feel they have outgrown Playtime products, but they are to be strongly discouraged from this notion. Their attachment to our characters and products should be maintained while they are living here, and we also discourage them from making "dark" interpretations of our characters.

SCHOOLHOUSE

The Playcare orphans receive all their education here, ranging from kindergarten to high school. Recently, Stella Greyber and Leith Pierre have overhauled the curriculum in an exciting way, adding more content concerning Playtime Co. itself. It's important the orphans know about the company's history and philosophy and the role Playtime Co.'s played in their lives. Their loyalty is very important to us!

We also want the orphans to understand what's involved in true innovation, and that it doesn't come without a cost. If we want a better future, we have to make some sacrifices! They're never too young to learn that.

PLAYTIME MADE A DOLL THAT WAS A TEACHER, AND WE USED THIS AS A MODEL FOR THE SCHOOLHOUSE'S TEACHER TOYS. THESE WERE THOUGHT TO BE CHEAPER, MORE RELIABLE, AND EASIER TO WORK WITH THAN ACTUAL TEACHERS. REAL TEACHERS MIGHT BE QUESTIONING SOME OF THE CONTENT THAT'S BEEN PUT ON THE CURRICULUM NOW.

PLAYHOUSE

This is a place where the children can hang out and play during breaks from the school day. Playtime Co. toys are available for them to play with. Note that the orphans are no longer permitted to bring toys made by other companies when they come under our care. If employees see any toys from other brands while working here, they are to remove them.

AND THE KIDS ARE NOT ALLOWED TO ASK WHAT HAPPENED TO THEIR OLD TOYS, EVER. IF THEY MENTION IT, EVERYONE PRETENDS LIKE THE TOY NEVER EXISTED. "BARBIE? THERE'S NO SUCH THING."

COUNSELORS' OFFICES

Our counselors act as parental figures for the orphans, looking after their day-to-day needs. Counseling sessions for our traumatized and sensitive orphans take place here, and this is also where we store files on the children.

These files contain sensitive information, so please don't read them! We know they're very interesting (some of those orphans have unbelievable backstories), but they should not be read without the explicit permission of Stella Greyber, whose office is also located here.

I'M NOT SURE WHICH OF THE COUNSELORS KNOW ABOUT THE EXPERIMENTS. THE MOST SENIOR ONES DO, I THINK. ONLY SPECIFIC COUNSELORS TAKE THE CHILDREN TO AND FROM THE GAME STATION AND REPORT BACK ABOUT THEIR PERFORMANCE AND SCHOOLWORK. MAYBE THE OTHERS DON'T KNOW WHAT IT'S ALL REALLY ABOUT.

SURELY THEY MUST HAVE FIGURED SOMETHING STRANGE WAS GOING ON—ALL THE ORPHANS WHO SUDDENLY FIND NEW HOMES AND MOVE OUT. I GUESS PEOPLE WANT TO THINK THEY'RE DOING GOOD IN THE WORLD, AND ON THE SURFACE, PLAYCARE LOOKS LIKE A GOOD THING.

Incident Report

Date: 11/20
Confidential For Science Team eyes only

Employee information

Name: P.W.
Department: Science

Incident details

Following placement within his new body, Subject 1188 was contained to allow him a slight "adjustment" period. However, a security team failed to properly secure and lock his cell. They attempted to confine Subject 1188 after he broke loose and utilized several tranquilizer darts in order to subdue him. Their eventual success came at the cost of six lives, whom Subject 1188 hunted individually.

The aftermath of this massacre was like a scene out of a horror movie, all blood and bodies along the corridors, tinged with tufts of purple fur.

REJECTED

Moving forward, we NEED to create stricter safety protocols for experimentation. Losing people like this is wasteful, both in terms of company resources and the valuable lives that were lost. We respect the importance of the work and its intended outcome, but if we want to keep our work moving according to schedule, we can't continue to divvy it up to the survivors and expect to keep the same pace or maintain morale.

These were our friends. Our teammates.

* Nicole Calloway
* Carter Stephens
* Douglas McKinty
* Dakota Geisler
* William Kole
* Trenton Roebke

Remember those names. They were people. Not things, people.

REJECTED

IT DIDN'T STOP WITH THEM. NOT AT ALL. NOTHING WAS DONE, AND NOTHING WILL BE DONE. THAT'S JUST WHAT WE HAVE TO LIVE WITH.

I'd be happy to sit with upper management and detail my ideas for safety improvements to better avoid these situations in the future. I won't see another teammate die.

DW

TRAIN STATION

Not to be confused with the Game Station train! This one is much less fun, we're afraid. It's a small subway system that takes employees to different parts of the factory. But it helps get you around quickly and saves your energy for work! The train station also has an Arcade Room, as part of our commitment to fun.

AFTER THE . . . INCIDENT, LEITH PIERRE PUT TOGETHER RESOURCE EXTRACTION TEAMS TO COLLECT PARTS THAT GOT SCATTERED ACROSS THE FACTORY IN THE CHAOS. IT WAS NOT SAFE TO DO THAT, BUT THEY WERE STILL TRYING TO RUN THE FACTORY LIKE IT WAS A BUSINESS AND NOT A DEATH TRAP. THE TRAIN IS THE ONLY WAY TO MOVE AROUND THE BUILDING QUICKLY NOW!

I SHOULD MAKE A NOTE ABOUT THE FEEDING PIT. IT'S A SECTION OF ABANDONED SEWER SYSTEMS WITH ALL THESE UNUSED PIPES IN THE WALLS. THIS IS WHERE THE WUGGYS LIVE—AS IN, FERAL MINI HUGGYS.

THERE IS NO WAY TO GET OUT OF THE FEEDING PIT, NOT BY YOURSELF! SO YOU CAN ONLY HOPE PEOPLE LIKE YOU ENOUGH TO PULL YOU OUT IF YOU HAPPEN TO FALL IN.

nsure
agreements sig   actual   pany.
Non-compliance will result in termination.

THEATER

This is an important part of the tours, as we put on performances here featuring our popular characters and we can also screen films. At the moment, these performances only take place at the factory, but who knows, maybe one day we'll take them on tour and unleash our Playtime pals on the wider world!

Other attractions of the Theater include a large Huggy Wuggy statue in front of the ticket desk, as well as statues of Bron, Kissy Missy, and others. We're currently renovating it to add exciting new areas.

For those conducting tours, remember to check to be sure any children haven't hidden in any of the Port-A-Lounges, and make sure they don't sneak backstage. We don't want to spoil the magic for them!

Snacks available in the lobby include character-branded items like Boogie Bites, Dino Dots, PJ Puffs, and Huggy Bricks. These are exclusive to the tour experience. You can't buy them anywhere outside the factory!

Please note we are **not** currently looking to hire any new performers to play the roles of our characters in the show. We've made arrangements for this that we think will work well for the company going forward.

1

P.C.U.S.S. - 48.1.142

Memo

From: Human Resources
To: Security
Re: Rowan Stoll

On March 30, 1991, an employee in the IT department, Rowan Stoll, contacted Leith Pierre, saying tour guests had been complaining the Huggy Wuggy statue seemed to be looking at them. Rowan believed there might be cameras installed in Huggy's eyes: "Look, if some . . . creep is hiding nanny cams in our mascot's eyeballs, this thing needs to be taken seriously."

On May 28, 1991, Rowan totally backtracked on all this, telling Leith a maintenance guy had simply not locked Huggy's eyes in place, so they appeared to be moving. He assured Leith he would cause no further problems: "I'm not looking into it any more . . . I mean, not like there was anything to look into in the first place. That's in the past. You won't be hearing anything else, uh, from me."

However, Rowan did not drop the matter and made a recording on which he claimed someone had tried to kill him, and he was going to release confidential information: "Next week, I've scheduled the company's servers, the security, to be shut down for sixty minutes of maintenance. While security is out, I can release everything and run. I think they are going to kill me first."

We recommend steps are taken to deal with this employee.

ROWAN'S DEATH WAS
CAUGHT ON TAPE. HE WAS
BOXY'S FIRST VICTIM.

PRODUCTION LINE

The Make-A-Friend machine can't cope with all the demands of manufacturing Playtime Co. products, and this area contains much of the machinery we use for this.

NEED TO SHUT IT ALL OUT?

In several areas of the factory, we've introduced another of our great, original ideas: the Port-A-Lounge. These may look like ordinary equipment lockers painted in bright colors, and that's exactly what they are. If you feel overwhelmed by your responsibilities, or a colleague is driving you crazy, step into a Port-A-Lounge for a mental health break. Stay in there as long as you need to!*

*For breaks longer than five minutes, your pay will be docked. No more than one break is to be taken per four-hour shift. Please do not scream while inside the Port-A-Lounge.

AH, THE PORT-A-LOUNGE, MY
OLD FRIEND. I MAKE USE OF
THESE PRETTY REGULARLY
WORKING IN THE LABS. IN
FACT, THERE IS OFTEN A
WAITING LIST TO USE THEM.
ONE OF THEM LITERALLY
SAVED MY LIFE ONCE...

DESTROY-A-TOY

We don't want rejected or faulty toys getting out into the world where they could do serious harm to the reputation of Playtime Co. or result in a lawsuit. So instead of just throwing them in the trash, where they might get picked out, given away, or resold, we have the Destroy-A-Toy facility!

Here, unwanted toys can be incinerated using flame- and lava-creating devices. It gets very hot in here, but we must emphasize this is **not** an excuse to work in your underwear. All employees **must** wear shirts and pants at all times. We don't want to have to remind you again.

You may think it's strange to devote such a large area of the factory to destroying toys. But it's just another one of those things we do differently here! We take destruction **very** seriously.

SOMEONE PUT A NOTE IN THE EMPLOYEE SUGGESTION BOX SAYING WE SHOULD INCLUDE THIS ON THE TOUR AND LET KIDS THROW TOYS INTO THE LAVA. I THINK SOME OF THE EXECUTIVES WERE IN FAVOR BECAUSE IT WOULD MEAN WE DIDN'T HAVE TO EMPLOY AS MANY PEOPLE TO WORK THE INCINERATORS IF WE COULD GET KIDS DOING IT FOR FREE. OTHERS THOUGHT WE SHOULDN'T ENCOURAGE KIDS TO SEE OUR TOYS AS TRASH TO BE BURNED. I CAN SEE BOTH ANGLES.

SCREENING ROOM

This is a relaxing environment where employees can watch and absorb our informational VHS tapes about aspects of the factory and the company's history. You are encouraged to take your breaks here.

PLAYTIME LOVES PUTTING INSTRUCTIONS ON TAPE FOR US. I GUESS THEY DON'T TRUST EVERYONE TO ACTUALLY READ THE EMPLOYEE HANDBOOK.

THERE ARE ALWAYS PLENTY OF TAPES AROUND, SO IT'S UNDERSTANDABLE THAT WHEN PEOPLE GOT CONCERNED ABOUT WHAT WAS GOING ON HERE AND WANTED TO MAKE A RECORD OF IT, THEY STARTED REUSING THE TAPES. PEOPLE RECORDED THINGS AND MADE MORE COPIES, HOPING THE TRUTH WOULD GET OUT SOMEHOW. THAT'S WHAT ROWAN STOLL THOUGHT, OBVIOUSLY.

1995

Playtime ℗ CO.

APRIL

1
2
3
4
5
6 ☆ INTERVIEW WITH
7   LOCAL POLICE
8   -DON'T FORGET
   KICKBACK MONEY
9
0
1
2
3 ☆ TEAM DEBRIEF
4
5
6
7 ☆ DEADLINE TO RESPOND
8   TO LAWSUITS-HAVE
9   BEEN TOLD TO DENY
   EVERYTHING
0
1
2
3
4
5
6
7
8
9
0

MAY

01 ☆ ~~SAFETY SEMINAR~~
02 ↖
03   CANCELED DUE
04   TO OUTBREAK OF
05   TOXIC GAS IN
  SEMINAR ROOM
06
07
08
09
10
11   SURGERY. REMEMBER TO
12   BRING CHANGE OF
13   CLOTHES AFTER WHAT
  HAPPENED LAST TIME
14 ↗
15 ☆
16 ☆ ↘
17   BOOKED FULL DAY IN
18   PORT-A-LOUNGE
19
20
21
22
23
24
25
26
27 ☆ DATA ENTRY WITH DR. SAWYER
28
29
30
31

JUNE

01
02
03
04
05
06
07
08
09 ☆   DEMONSTRATION
10   FOR TOY STORE BUYERS
11   LOOKING AHEAD TO
12   CHRISTMAS
13   -VERY HIGH
   SECURITY
14
15
16
17
18 ☆ MEETING TO DISCUSS CONCERNS
   FROM PLAYCARE STAFF
19 ☆ MEETING TO DISCUSS CONCERNS
   FROM GAME STATION STAFF
20
21 ☆ MEETING TO DISCUSS CONCERNS
   FROM INNOVATION STAFF
22 ☆ MEETING TO DISCUSS CONCERNS
   FROM SECURITY STAFF
23 ☆ MEETING TO DISCUSS CONCERNS
   FROM ALL OTHER STAFF
24
25
26
27
28 ☆IT'S YOUR BIRTHDAY!
29
30

139

EMPLOYEE CALENDAR

JULY

01
02
03 ☆ CONSTRUCTION REVIEW OF NEW HOLDING CELLS
04
05
06
07 ☆ EVALUATION OF LABS
08
09
10
11
12 ☆ ~~COMPANY AWAY DAY~~
13
14 ↖ CANCELLED
15
16
17
18 ☆ MEETING ABOUT
19   CHANGES TO
20   PLAYCARE SCHEDULE
21
22
23
24
25
26
27   CANCELED DUE
28   TO DEEPLY
29   UNSETTLING NOISES
30   IN SEMINAR ROOM
31 ↖
☆ ~~SAFETY SEMINAR~~

AUGUST

01
02
03 ☆ ~~QUITTING!~~
04 ↙
05   HAVE BEEN
06   PERSUADED
07   TO STAY
08 ☆ NEW PLAYCARE
09   SCHEDULE COMES IN
10
11
12
13
14
15
16
17
18
19
20
21
22
23
24
25
26
27
28
29
30
31

SEPTEMBE

01
02
03
04
05
06
07
08
09
10
11
12
13
14
15
16
17
18
19
20
21
22
23
24
25
26
27
28
29
30

1995

Playtime™

OCTOBER

1
2
3
4
5
6
7
8
9
0
1
2
3
4
5
6
7
8
9
0
1
2
3
4
5
6
7
8
9
0
1

NOVEMBER

01
02
03
04
05
06
07
08
09
10
11
12
13
14
15
16
17
18
19
20
21
22
23
24
25
26
27
28
29
30

DECEMBER

01
02
03
04
05
06
07
08
09
10
11
12
13
14
15
16
17
18
19
20
21
22
23
24
25
26
27
28
29
30
31

EMPLOYEE QUIZ

We hope you've been paying attention!

Scoring less than 70 percent on this quiz may result in termination of your employment at Playtime Co. Good luck!

1) When was Playtime Co. founded?
2) How many legs does PJ Pugapillar have?
3) What pendant does CatNap wear?
4) What is KickinChicken's favorite activity?
5) How much did Poppy Playtime cost when she launched?
6) What name was Kick-Me-Paul resubmitted under?
7) What does the yellow GrabPack hand do?
8) What days do tours take place?
9) How many fuses operate the control panel in Storage and Supply?
10) Which toy does the Make-A-Friend machine make?
11) What two colors are added in the third round of Musical Memory?
12) Which room does the Bunzo Bunny production line run through?
13) Which component in the Incinerating Room often needs replacing?
14) Who is the head of Playcare?
15) What are the names of two snacks that are available in the Theater?

QUIZ ANSWERS

1) 1930

2) 44

3) A moon

4) Skateboarding

5) $5.99

6) Push-Me-Paul

7) Launches the user into the air

8) Wednesdays, Thursdays, and Fridays

9) Four

10) Cat-Bee

11) White and orange

12) C2

13) The gear

14) Stella Greyber

15) Any two: Boogie Bites, Dino Dots, PJ Puffs, or Huggy Bricks